SWEET STUFF

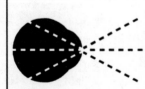

This Large Print Book carries the
Seal of Approval of N.A.V.H.

1 Introduction

Climate is what you expect.
Weather is what you get.
                    Anon.

Weather and climate variability

Every year there are extreme climate-related problems around the globe, with droughts occurring in some places and floods in others. For example, the summer of 1988 witnessed a severe drought in the agricultural heartland of North America and extremely low streamflow in the basin of the mighty Mississippi River. Just a few years later, in the summer of 1993, a period of very heavy rains led to major flooding along the Upper Mississippi and Lower Missouri rivers and many of their tributaries in the United States Midwest. In the early 1990s, newspaper headlines noted that drought-related food shortages in southern Africa put about 80 million Africans at risk of famine. In early 1995, extreme flooding occurred in western Europe, shaking the confidence of countries such as the Netherlands in their ability to prevent natural catastrophes, and challenging their false belief that scientific and technological developments had buffered their societies from the consequences of such periods of extremely heavy rainfall. This was not unlike the situation in the 1970s and 1980s, when Canadian officials sought to "drought-proof" the climate-sensitive agricultural areas in the Canadian prairie provinces, only to realize the impossibility of such a daunting task.

The point is that record-setting climate events are occurring somewhere in the world each year. In fact, Sir John Houghton, head of a major international program designed to assess the level of present understanding of the science of climate change, has suggested that "records are being set every year and if there were a year without such an occurrence, that in itself would be record-setting." (J. T. Houghton, cited by Greenpeace International, 1994).

Nevertheless, it seems that in some years there are many more extreme meteorological events and resulting societal problems, such as droughts, floods, frosts, or blizzards, than one might expect, even if they were not record-setting. One such period was 1972–73, when severe droughts occurred in widely dispersed locations such as Australia and Indonesia, Brazil and Central America, India and in parts of sub-Saharan Africa, and heavy flooding occurred in Kenya, southern Brazil, and parts of Ecuador and Peru. At that time it was suggested that some of these widely dispersed climatic extremes might have had a common geographic origin – changes in sea surface temperatures in the Pacific Ocean (El Niño or EN) and changes in sea level atmospheric pressure across the Pacific basin (the Southern Oscillation or SO). These combined changes have come to be commonly referred to as El Niño events in the popular media and as ENSO (El Niño–Southern Oscillation) events in much of the scientific literature.

Very briefly, an El Niño event can be described as the appearance from time to time of warm sea surface water in the central and eastern Pacific Ocean near the equator. Folklore suggests that the term "El Niño" (literally, the Spanish phrase for "the Christ Child" or "Baby Jesus") was used by Peruvian fishermen who had noticed the annual appearance of warm water along the western coast by December of each year. In some years, the warming along the coast did not dissipate within the usual few months but lingered for more than a year. This too was called "El Niño." "El Niño" has now been broadened to include all kinds of sea surface warming in the equatorial Pacific. Scientists believe that El Niño events are related to anomalous weather extremes around the globe.

During the past couple of decades the public has learned of El Niño and its impacts in a sporadic way. It would be mentioned in the popular media only when a big El Niño event was believed to be under way. Many of those articles or news releases were simply reports of the events of the day and were devoid of in-depth discussion of the phenomenon. Once the El Niño event (or threat of it) had passed, the media's interest in it waned rapidly. One of the key reasons for undertaking the preparation of this book is to provide a user-friendly account of what El Niño is, what it does and why we, as members of different societies, need to have more than a passing, intermittent interest in it, limited for the most part to when it occurs every few years or so.

El Niño and worldwide climate

The associations between El Niño events and unusual changes in normal climate patterns (called anomalies) around the globe have been referred to by scientists as "teleconnections." These are known, as well as alleged, connections between El Niño events and changes in distant weather or climate-related processes. For example, there appears to be an association between El Niño events and droughts in various parts of the globe:

northern Australia, southeastern Africa, Northeast Brazil, parts of India, Central America, and so forth. There also appear to be linkages between El Niño events and a reduced number of tropical hurricanes occurring in a given year along the east coast of the USA as well as in the locations of tropical cyclones off the east coast of Australia, where they tend to shift equatorward by several hundred kilometers.

One location where ecosystems and human activities are known to be directly and, for the most part, adversely affected by El Niño is the area along the western coast of South America, specifically Peru, Ecuador, and northern Chile. Just about every event, regardless of whether weak or strong, has an impact on this region.

El Niño and societal impacts

El Niño is a natural phenomenon that recurs every few years. To varying degrees, it affects a large portion of the world's population. Potentially useful scientific information about El Niño and its impacts on society will probably go unused, unless there are sustained efforts to educate the public about how to realize the value of seemingly abstract scientific research findings. For this reason alone, it is important for the general public, for managers in various economic sectors, and for policymakers to know more about the El Niño phenomenon, including its teleconnections, and its implications for ecosystems and societies around the globe. The scientific literature and popular media are full of statements about the value to society of being forewarned about the possible onset of an El Niño. On an idealized, abstract level, it is not difficult to find value in forecasts of El Niño events or, for that matter, forecasts of any climate-related environmental change. However, when it comes to a specific El Niño event and its specific impacts in local areas worldwide, it becomes a highly speculative endeavor to place a precise value on such forecasts.

El Niño and Peru

The value of knowing more about El Niño to various sectors of Peruvian society has been mentioned in general statements since at least the end of the 1800s. For example, at an International Geographical Congress held in Lima, Peru, in the early 1890s, Peruvian geographer Federico Alfonzo Pezet stated that

> the existence of this counter-current [El Niño] is a known fact, and what is now wanted is that proper and definite studies, surveys, and observations should be undertaken in order to get to the bottom of the question, and

find out everything relating to this counter-current, and to the influence which it appears to exercise in the regions where its action is most felt.

(Pezet, 1895, p. 605)

One of the major regional influences Pezet referred to was heavy rainfall that extended well beyond a single season in northern Peru that usually accompanied El Niño events.

One could easily argue that, at the end of the nineteenth century, El Niño was of interest mainly to local populations along the western coast of South America because of the associated disruptions in both normal (i.e., expected) rainfall patterns and reproductive and behavioral patterns of fish and bird populations along the coast. Actually, concern was not so much directed toward the apparent adverse impacts on fish as it was toward the bird populations that lived off them.

During major El Niño events, fish populations, especially anchoveta, would be reduced as a result of decreased food supply and would shift their location, becoming less accessible to fish-eating birds. As a direct result, millions of adult sea birds and their chicks would perish. The carcasses of thousands of dead birds would wash up onto Peruvian beaches. In many countries, the occasional high level of mortality among bird populations might receive brief notoriety; not so for the sea birds of Peru. Various sea birds earned the name of guano birds because they were highly valued in Peru for their excrement (called guano). Guano was "discovered" by European chemists in the early 1800s to be rich in nitrogen and phosphorus. It was to be used as an excellent fertilizer for agricultural fields in Britain, Europe, and the USA. Guano was considered a valuable export commodity for Peru between 1840 and 1880. El Niño-related reductions in the guano bird population led to reduced production of guano in Peru's guano-bird rookeries on the rocky Chincha Islands and coastal areas (Figure 1.1).

El Niño and the world

Because of the advent of manufactured fertilizers and other trade-related factors, Peru's ability to export guano waned and, as a result, birds and guano production were no longer major generators of Peruvian concern about El Niño or its ecological impacts. Interest in El Niño shifted in the 1950s to the exploitation of the anchoveta fish population for the purpose of fishmeal production. With the collapse of that fishery in the mid-1970s, the health of fish populations in the eastern equatorial Pacific no longer generated global interest in El Niño episodes. Primary interest today centers on the realization that El Niño is a Pacific basin-wide

Figure 1.1. The rocky islands along the coast of Peru provide nesting sites for "guano" birds. In the absence of an El Niño event, the birds are highly productive, consuming large quantities of fish, primarily anchoveta, that dwell near the ocean's surface. This is converted into guano, bird droppings that are used as a fertilizer for agriculture. When the warm waters appear in the region, signaling an El Niño (warm) event, the fish become fewer in number and are dispersed, becoming inaccessible to the birds. (Jaime Jahncke – IMARPE.)

phenomenon with regional perturbations of climate- and weather-related processes throughout most of the world.

Increasingly, the task of understanding El Niño is seen by climatologists and meteorologists as an important key to unlocking mysteries about tropical climate and weather patterns and, to a varying extent, their impacts on regions outside the tropics (called the extra-tropics). In fact, an increasing number of El Niño researchers now claim that they can reliably forecast the onset of El Niño. Depending on the particular researcher, claims for lead time (i.e., advanced warning) range from four to 12 months. Some of these claims are considered to be realistic and have, in turn, captured the attention of policymakers who continue to support physical science research on El Niño and forecasting efforts in a major way. Disruptions of regional climate patterns and of human activities during El Niño events reinforce the need for development of reliable, long-range, climate-related forecasts, which can then be used to reduce the impacts on society and on vulnerable ecosystems of climate and weather extremes.

El Niño and international science

Scientific research interest in El Niño has blossomed. El Niño research is no longer left to Peruvian scientists interested in sea birds or fish to investigate the phenomenon only for its adverse, local ecological consequences. Now, they have been joined by a small army of scientific researchers, drawn from all continents and from several academic disciplines, who are actively engaged in individual as well as collaborative research on El Niño-related topics. Their shared expectation is to resolve lingering mysteries about the phenomenon and to uncover the underlying mechanisms that perpetuate El Niño events and govern their life cycles. Such discoveries would probably enable scientists to forecast El Niño with a high degree of reliability several months to a year in advance of the onset, growth, and decay phases of the phenomenon.

Today, policymakers who have been funding science are asking questions about the value to society of its work. With limited national budgets, researchers are having to consider the usability of their research findings. Forecasting El Niño and, more broadly, the forecasting of climate variability from one year to the next, has potential benefits to society. El Niño research can easily be used to demonstrate how the scientific community can produce "usable science." The scientific community has only recently come to realize the need for sustained efforts to educate the public, and especially policymakers, about the importance of this phenomenon. There has also been a sharp increase in policymaker interest in identifying the environmental and societal consequences of El Niño.

El Niño as a "living" thing

Like many other processes in nature, El Niño comes and goes again and again. Like other recurring phenomena in nature, such as seasonal vegetation cycles, mountain snowpack, glacial advance and retreat, and sand dune movement, El Niño events wax and wane over time in their responses to climatic fluctuations.

As with any attempt to discuss a system with many interacting components, identifying the best place to begin is often difficult. For example, how might one best describe the human body? Before discussing the parts of the human body and their functions, one must have an idea of how the body as a whole works. By analogy, for El Niño it is necessary to describe the phenomenon (i.e., the body) and then to describe its components and their various interactions. In using such an approach, however, it is difficult to avoid some repetition. This inconvenience aside, the reader will gain a better picture of El Niño and its impacts on weather and climate anomalies around the globe.

The word "complex"

The scientific community relies heavily on the use of the term "complex." Atmospheric processes are complex; so too are oceanic processes. El Niño is the result of complex interactions between the atmosphere and the ocean. In reality everything is complex, from the electron that circles the nucleus of an atom to the far reaches of the universe.

However, in addition to the acceptance of scientific complexity, the term "complex" has also been used for a variety of other reasons. For example, "complex" has been used as an adjective to suggest that an understanding of the phenomenon under investigation cannot be known in its entirety. It has also been used to suggest that it will take a long time (i.e., much money) to understand it completely. "Complex" has also been used by scientists as a caveat to note "buyer beware"; that the users of such information should treat it as imperfect information. In some instances, it has been used to suggest that you (the reader) cannot possibly understand all that the scientist could tell you about the phenomenon, so he/she won't bother to try. In sum, the notion of complexity can be used, on the one hand, to expose the limits to our depth of knowledge or, on the other hand, to hide our ignorance. In this book the term will be used sparingly, assuming that readers are well aware of just how complicated are various natural processes and interactions. How much of the science of El Niño does the non-expert *need* to know? How much detail can be left out or generalized in a description of processes and events, while the account still conveys an understanding that is correct, even if not complete? That is the challenge of those who seek to write about scientific issues for those of us who are not physical scientists.

Chapter overview

Chapter 2 presents definitions of El Niño and brings to light a main source of the confusion that surrounds the phenomenon. It attempts to provide a broad definition for El Niño. Chapter 3, entitled "A tale of two histories," presents a brief history of the emergence and spread of scientific interest in El Niño and in the Southern Oscillation.

The fourth chapter, "Biography of El Niño," describes various characteristics and processes associated with El Niño and the Southern Oscillation and Chapter 5 discusses the 1982–83 event, which has been considered the biggest in a century. Attention is drawn to the importance for scientific research of the 1972–73 event.

Chapter 6 considers the value, in theory and in practice, of "Forecasting El Niño," providing a few examples of forecast successes and failures. Also mentioned is the unexpected behavior of air–sea interactions in the equatorial Pacific in the 1991–95 period, as well as the need for an international institute for climate prediction on an interannual basis.

Many people are interested in the equatorial Pacific, insofar as they believe that their regional climate is affected by events there. Chapter 7 focuses on the linkages of weather or climate anomalies in distant locations, called teleconnections, believed to be associated with El Niño.

How researchers monitor, investigate and forecast El Niño events is briefly discussed in Chapter 8, and Chapter 9 outlines some of the major post-war international science programs, starting with the International Geophysical Year (1957–58) and extending into the beginning of the next century. This chapter also addresses questions raised about how global warming of the atmosphere might affect El Niño events. If the atmosphere were to warm by a few degrees Celsius in the last half of the next century, that would probably affect the El Niño process in as yet unknown ways.

Why care about El Niño? is addressed in Chapter 10, which suggests why people who are not directly affected by its effects should also take interest in the phenomenon. The specific examples provided suggest that there are costs associated with not using El Niño information that is already available and considered reliable.

The eleventh chapter is a collection of thoughts by researchers whose activities span several decades. These scientists represent various disciplines and activities and they were asked to provide a few paragraphs about an aspect of El Niño that he or she wished to share with the readers.

The final chapter addresses the contentious issue of "Usable Science," what it is and who decides which research findings are of direct use to society on a time scale of interest to present-day decisionmakers.

The crossword puzzle (Figure 1.2, overleaf) is based on the El Niño phenomenon. While most readers would have trouble at the outset answering the puzzle's clues, it is hoped that they will be able to attack it after having read *Currents of change: El Niño's impact on climate and society*.

ACROSS

1. One of the Southern Oscillation's northern sisters
3. Decade-long research program on Pacific air–sea interaction
6. Researcher associated with Niño 3
8. Highly productive oceanic regions
13. Statistical measure for identifying teleconnections
14. Concept used to manage fisheries
15. Fishmeal production by-product
16. Peru's fishing rival
20. 1970s biological experiment on coastal upwelling
21. Shares ecological niche with anchoveta
22. He identified the Southern Oscillation
26. Spanish word for "here"
28. Measure of equatorial Pacific pressure changes
30. Pressure pattern affecting North American weather
31. Major producer of fishmeal
32. Fishing net characteristic determining the size of fish that can be caught
33. Limits the movement of internal (Kelvin) waves
36. Prestigious US scientific academy
39. Synthetic fiber that revolutionized fishing in Peru
40. He identified the link between the EN and the SO
41. Word for metric ton

DOWN

2. Animal feed supplement source taken from the sea
3. Linkage between remote climate anomalies and El Niño
4. He created an historical time series of El Niño events
5. An alleged by-product of El Niño-related drought in Indonesia
7. El Niño's other name
9. University of Hawaii professor who measured sea level changes with tide gauges in the equatorial Pacific
10. The opposite of El Niño's cold event
11. Site of the first major workshop on El Niño in the mid-1970s
12. South-to-north circulation pattern in the Pacific
16. Site of Peru's Marine Institute
17. Rainfall failures in this country prompted search for teleconnections
18. Location used in the Southern Oscillation Index
19. Site of the Earth Summit in June 1992
21. Fish off Pacific Northwest coast affected by El Niño events
23. The Christ Child
24. Thermal reservoir in the western Pacific Ocean
25. Primary use of Peruvian anchovy
27. Spanish word for "what"
29. Peru's research center concerned with effects of El Niño
34. Fertilizer; bird excrement
35. Program created by four western South American countries to assess El Niño impacts
37. A second-choice animal feed if fishmeal is unavailable
38. A change in this ocean characteristic signals the onset of an El Niño (abbreviation)

Figure 1.2. Solving the El Niño mystery. Crossword puzzle by M. H. Glantz. All terms in the El Niño crossword puzzle are referred to in the text. The solution may be found on p. 188.

Section I
Emerging interest in El Niño

2 El Niño

El Niño definitions

The term "El Niño" means different things to different people. In Spanish, *el niño* means small boy or child. With capital letters, El Niño refers to Jesus as an infant. To Peruvians, it has an additional meaning: a particular intermittent warm ocean current that moves southward along its coast. They gave the ocean current the name El Niño at some time before the beginning of the twentieth century, although its exact origin and "birth date" remain unknown. The popular contemporary version of how it got its name relates to the fact that warm waters appear off the coast of Peru seasonally, beginning around Christmas time (i.e., during the Southern Hemisphere summer, which is the Northern Hemisphere winter), temporarily replacing the usually cold waters in that region for a few months. The normally cold waters along the coast are the result of coastal upwelling processes by which deep, cold, nutrient-rich water wells up to the ocean's sunlit surface (called the euphotic zone).

At a Geography Society meeting in Lima in 1892, Peruvian navy captain Camilo Carrillo was apparently the source of information (and rumor) about how the El Niño current got its name. He made the following statement, which has now been repeated many times:

> Peruvian sailors from the port of Paita in northern Peru, who frequently navigate along the coast in small crafts, either to the north or to the south of Paita, named this current "El Niño" without doubt because it is most noticeable and felt after Christmas.
>
> (Carrillo, 1892, p. 84)

Occasionally, the seasonally warmer water that appeared off the coast of Peru and Ecuador (a region referred to as the eastern equatorial Pacific) would linger longer than a few months, sometimes lasting well into the following year. These prolonged "invasions" (more correctly, appearances) of warm water have led to pronounced disruptions of regional coastal ecosystems and socioeconomic activities.

In his speech to the International Geographical Congress in Lima, Pezet

(1895, p. 605) noted: "that this hot current has caused the great rainfalls in the rainless regions of Peru appears a fact, as it has been observed that these heavy rains have taken place during the summers of excessive heat". Even though we do not know when El Niño events were recognized as such, we do know that they have occurred over millennia, as the impact of heavy rains and flooding has left its marks on the natural environment in Peru and Equador.

As of the beginning of the twentieth century, the connection between the occurrence of El Niño and the various changes in the natural environment around the tropics, from the east coast of the African continent to the west coast of South America, had not yet been made. El Niño's impacts were only of concern in Peru and Ecuador, where they were considered to be local manifestations of a local oceanic or atmospheric variation.

As early as the mid-1970s, El Niño had acquired several definitions (Barnett, 1977). By the mid-1990s, several dozen El Niño definitions could be found in scientific articles and books, ranging from simple to complex ones. The following two definitions serve as examples.

> El Niño: A 12–18 month period during which anomalously warm sea surface temperatures occur in the eastern half of the equatorial Pacific. Moderate or strong El Niño events occur irregularly, about once every 5–6 years or so on average.
>
> (Gray, 1993)

> Originally ... an El Niño referred to warm current flows along the coasts of Ecuador and Peru in January, February, and March, and the resulting impact on local weather. ... The second name, ENSO, more generally refers to events from the mid-Pacific to the South American coast, taking into account the irregular oscillation in pressure between the east and west Pacific.
>
> (Palca, 1986)

However, some common aspects of El Niño do recur in these definitions. El Niño

- is an anomalous warming of surface water,
- appears off the coasts of Ecuador and northern Peru (sometimes Chile),
- is linked to changes in pressure at sea level across the Pacific Ocean (Southern Oscillation),
- recurs but not at regular intervals,
- involves sea surface temperature increases in the eastern and central Pacific,
- is a warm southward-flowing current off the coast of Peru,
- accompanies a slackening of westward-flowing equatorial trade winds,